Original concept by
Roger Hargreaves

Written and illustrated by
Adam Hargreaves

EGMONT

Mr Birthday could not believe his bad luck.

He had caught a cold.

It was such bad timing.

He had Mr Silly's birthday party to organise.

Which was a problem.

And to make matters worse, Little Miss Helpful had just arrived ...

Little Miss Helpful wanted to be as helpful as possible, but, somehow or other, things never quite turned out as she meant them to.

"Here's a nice bowl of soup for you," she announced, but, somehow or other, she tripped on the rug and then, somehow or other, she knocked into the chair and then, somehow or other, the bowl of soup landed on Mr Birthday's head.

And to top it all, somehow or other, Mr Birthday had accepted Little Miss Helpful's offer to organise Mr Silly's party.

Little Miss Helpful had insisted and Mr Birthday had not been able to say no.

"Oh dear," muttered Mr Birthday.

TO DO
LIST.

And, as Mr Birthday had feared, things began to unravel from the start.

Little Miss Helpful managed to ask all the wrong people to help.

She asked Little Miss Naughty to blow up the balloons.

But Little Miss Naughty was up to her usual tricks.

Little Miss Helpful asked Mr Forgetful to send the invitations.

She asked Mr Funny to make the jelly and ice cream.

She asked Mr Muddle to bake a birthday cake.

Little Miss Dotty was in charge of the pass-the-parcel parcel.

And she asked Mr Mean to buy a birthday present.

SHOP

The first sign of trouble was when Little Miss Helpful realised that nobody had received their invitation. Mr Forgetful had forgotten to put stamps on the envelopes.

It was then that Little Miss Helpful ran into Mr Noisy.

Mr Noisy climbed to the top of the hill and in his remarkably loud voice shouted across the countryside.

"YOU ARE ALL INVITED TO MR SILLY'S BIRTHDAY PARTY THIS AFTERNOON!"

And, with Mr Noisy's voice still ringing in their ears everyone turned up for the party.

Although, it was not quite the party that Little Miss Helpful had hoped for.

There were balloons. But they were water balloons.

There was jelly and ice cream served in wellington boots.

Jelly in wellies!

They played pass the castle!

No parcel.

No unwrapping.

And no surprise.

How dotty!

And the birthday cake was a birthday steak!

Everything went wrong.

And Mr Silly loved it all.

It was just as silly a birthday party as he could have hoped for.

He even liked Mr Mean's present.

One sock!

"Well," laughed Mr Birthday, who was feeling much better, "if you are lucky, you might get the other sock for your birthday next year."

"I hope it's a different colour," giggled Mr Silly.

"I like odd socks!"